Fair Oak Infant School

# Rock-pooling

Written by Emma Lynch

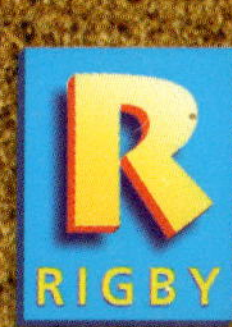

This is the coast.

We are going rock-pooling.

This is a rock pool.

The rock pool is deep.
Look at the floating weeds.

This is a shrimp net.

Look at this shrimp.
Shrimps are not big.

This is a crab.
Crabs are shellfish.

Look at the fish.
They are swimming.

This is a sailing boat.

See it float along.

Gulls sit high up on the rocks.

They swoop to get the food.

Wet shells look bright in the sun.

It is night at the coast.
The rock pool is still.

# Things we can see at the coast